Whispered Blessings

Stories that Inform, Illuminate and Inspire

Deborah T. Simon

W0010405

Whispered Blessings

ISBN: 978-1-935125-74-7

Cover illustration by Elizabeth Sue Orr
San Jose, CA

Cover design and book layout by Clarice Hirata
Hirata Design, Mt. View, CA   www.hiratadesign.com

Author's Photo by Bruce Holcomb
Shoot on Site Photography, San Mateo, CA

Printed in the United States of America on acid-free paper

For information or to purchase additional copies of this book go to:
www.rp-author.com/simon

Robertson Publishing
59 N. Santa Cruz Avenue, Suite B
Los Gatos, California 95030 USA
(888) 354-5957 • www.RobertsonPublishing.com

This first book I dedicate to
my first born,

Rahime Kewesi Simon,

and to my dear uncle,

Donald P. Stone,

both who remind me

that the impossible can be made possible.

"When it comes to acknowledgments and expressions of gratitude, let your heart lead you. Do not be shy or uncomfortable. Each expression of gratitude is a prayer. As your gratitude flows, so flow your blessings."

—Momma Tee

ACKNOWLEDGEMENTS

My overflowing gratitude to all who tended the garden of possibilities with me, stood with me when my courage faltered, sheltered me when the skies dripped ice and held me up when my commitment needed bolstering. And, blessings to all of you who reminded me that my vision of story is built on a strong foundation of faith.

My deepest gratitude and love to my dear, dear sisters who believed in me when I did not believe in myself. Sister, Yolanda S. Peeks for her straightforward direct comments and red pen and sister, Stephanie D. Simon for her absolute brilliance in guiding me back to my path when I veered off.

Endless appreciation to Karl Cishek, Judy Blanding-Borders, Ferial Hurst, Julie Painchaud, Mary Conroy, Sadhna Gupta, Anne Welker, Ann Hayes, Paul Johnannessen, Jahred Namasté, Kira Simon, Pat Kirti Hall, Priya Friday-Pabros, and the entire Recalling Spirit Ministries (RSM) Community for their faith, encouragement and patience. To Sue Orr, a delight and an incredible artist I bow to her for her willingness to collaborate with me and for coaxing the spirit of Momma Tee from the blank canvas and to Clarice Hirata of Hirata Design my new friend for bringing her considerable talent to the design and layout of this project.

Thanks to Chike Nwoffiah and Nancy Newlin for their excellent coaching, guidance and technical expertise toward taking the final draft and shaping it into a book.

Ophelia Saunders, Ma Dear, thank you for making everything so easy to understand and I give gratitude to God for giving us to each other at this time in our lives.

Endless respect, gratitude and love to my teacher, Rev. Ellen Grace O'Brian, Uma, Senior Minister and founder of the Center for Spiritual Enlightenment (CSE) in San Jose, CA for guiding me along the path of Kriya Yoga and for reminding me that, "All of our experiences have value and God makes use of everything."

I am humbled by this gift of story and my gratitude to Life is as boundless as the Universe; my prayer is always from the Bible, Psalm 19:14, "Let the words of my mouth, and the meditations of my heart, be acceptable in thy sight. . ."

In peace and love,
Deborah T. Simon

STORIES

INTRODUCTION

Grandparents whisper a blessing
in the ears of newly born babies,
". . . You can be whatever you want to be.
You can make the impossible possible . . ."

—Momma Tee

The impossible made possible is an idea, a principle, a mantra that was repeated to me over and over again throughout my childhood into my life as an adult. This mantra has been passed through my family throughout generations. Out of this mantra flows this compilation of stories that is a mixture of fact, fiction, and fantasy stirred with the tellers' imagination. Capturing the human experience, stories in this collection go beyond the boundaries of generations, culture and faith traditions.

I fell in love with stories listening to my elder sisters read to me—more times than I can count—*The Story of Live Dolls,* Momma Tee telling tales of strong queens and sharing the legend of a slight brown skinned woman facing down phantoms in the middle of the night and the anecdotal account of a Black man starting a school on the land that had been owned by former slave owners. Stories of the impossible being made possible, stories have always been a part of my life; stories are pivotal to my evolution.

The stories in this collection have been used to set the tenor for conferences and to bring meetings to a thought-full conclusion. These stories can be used in business settings to motivate, to instruct, to demonstrate how to overcome difficulties, and to illustrate success. *Mike and Phoebe, A Man Who Moved a Mountain,* and *The Legend of Susie Edwards* have been used at conferences and meetings, because the theme—the impossible is made possible—is repeated in each one.

Stories in this collection have been used in the political arena to demonstrate how with vision, courage, commitment, and faith change is possible. Each one of our elected representatives has a story of what motivated them to work on the behalf of all people. Politicians use stories as a vehicle to connect the issues, their philosophy, and their position to each individual voter. *A Man Who Moved a Mountain,* included in this collection, is a metaphor for an American's journey to move a simple, responsible, ethical legislative bill through a rocky uphill journey to adoption.

Educators and trainers have used stories from this collection to introduce a subject, to expand on a topic, to connect a student with their classmates and to entertain and delight the listener. A teacher reads a story and the students are captivated as each one listens to the story. The flexible teacher uses the story as a way to reach that child, or teen or adult who nods off or whose mind wanders during a lesson full of numbers, facts, and figures. The story is also a way to capture the attention of those who might be unresponsive to history told without the story.

Marie-Nathalie Beaudoin, PhD, training director at the Bay Area Family Therapy Associates (BAFTTA) in her second edition of *Responding to the Culture of Bullying & Disrespect,* uses *Bubble Trouble* to set up a discussion among educators about their beliefs and relationships about their own power.[1] Stories bring lessons to life; lessons learned from stories last a lifetime.

As ministry, the story is remembrance, an expression of gratitude and a celebration. All faith traditions are steeped in the remembrance of the Divine, that which is called many names yet cannot not be named, captured or defined within the context of our limited language. It is the story that sparks the transformation to living authentically as our selves; the story of human redemption, salvation, awakening; human transformation to the awareness that the Holy, the Sacred expresses as us. It is the story of human triumph over adversity that inspires us to *keep on keeping on.* The story is what moves us to open the door to *possibility* and stories of unconditional acceptance and love teach us how to embrace the other. The natural outflow of remembrance is gratitude; gratitude lifts us up then moves us to again remember our blessings. Every faith tradition has stories, rituals, celebrations and observations. Every tradition has rituals surrounding the birth of a child; *rites of passage* that mark the transformation from childhood to adulthood, sacred observances joining two people in marriage and holy customs marking the end of this life and the beginning of another. Stories of celebration are recalled though our rituals; stories of remembrance and gratitude remind us that life is a gift. *Whispered Blessings* stories inform, illuminate and inspire. These stories are ministry because they stir reflection, arouse gratitude and remind us to celebrate our blessings.

> *A good storyteller captures the listener's attention;*
> *a great storyteller engages the listener*
> *and makes the story theirs.*

> —Momma Tee

This journey through *Whispered Blessings* is a reflection and retelling of stories shared by Momma Tee. As the author of this collection, my role has been to imagine them in their fullness, capture them, and to write them down as quickly and as accurately as I can. Then share them with . . . everyone!

Momma Tee's walk was intentional and steady. "Our thoughts, words, and actions are living things; we must always consider their impact on all other living things." With brushes made of words, Momma Tee filled my mind's eye with delicious colors. The tempo of her words introduced my ears to rhythm and music that taught my imagination to play along. She knew and embraced her own power and she knew and used the power of the spoken and written word. She whispered a blessing in the ears of newly born babies,

> *You can be whatever you want to be.*
> *You can do whatever you believe you can do.*
> *If you have vision, if you are committed,*
> *And if you have courage and faith,*
> *You can make the impossible possible!*

> —Momma Tee

Telling stories and reading to children creates a bond that is difficult to break and if we get lost along the way, we can find our way home again through stories; they are for families seeking connection and love. This collection of stories is meant to be read aloud, to be shared, and to be used by everyone.

Teachers, tell your children all the stories, read to them; engage them in seeing how the journey has been traveled at another place and time. It is through the story that children explore possibilities, lay the world before them. Let their creativity fly—it is through the story and all of the arts in which children learn the essential quality of critical thinking. Parents, reading to your children and loving them unconditionally are among the most important things that you can do to prepare your child for the future that you will never see. The lessons, the messages, and the values that you share through stories will always stay with your children, becoming stories that they share with their children.

I give you these stories for your heart, your ears, and for your spirit. *Whispered Blessings* stories provide a welcome break, a brief vacation from the constant 24/7 grasping, pulling, and seeking pace of today's world. Some of the stories will tug at your heart. They may make you laugh, cry or stir you to reflection. These stories transcend faith, culture, gender, and generations. They are for anyone who has ever had an obstacle in their path, an ocean to cross, or a mountain to move. They are for those seeking inspiration, hope and a way to move beyond the familiar into the unknown.

Sit back, relax and let the stories ahead take you on a journey to possibility.

Mike and Phoebe is the story of love as a sacred trust, a commitment that could not be broken. It is a story that moves us to open the door to possibility.

Bubble Trouble engages children of all ages and demonstrates how just by using our minds we can turn something, anything, even a bubble into a whole lot of trouble.

The Legend of Susie Edwards is held in the Story Bowl. The Story Bowl holds our family's stories and has been in our family longer than our memories. Out of the Story Bowl pours a tale of strength and courage that has become one of our most enduring legends.

A Man Who Moved a Mountain is the journey of an ordinary boy who, over the course of a lifetime, transforms a vision into an extraordinary reality. It is the story of how one person taught generations that if you have vision and courage, if you are committed and have faith, then you too can make the impossible possible.

A Legacy: My Chat with a Nazi is a conversation between an African American woman and a Nazi. Impossible many have said, but the story demonstrates how through listening and a mutual willingness to let down barriers and remain open to possibility, how two people share a conversation that changes both of their lives.

Whispered Blessings is for all those who have asked me more times that I can count about Momma Tee. Through *Whispered Blessings* it is my pleasure to introduce you to Momma Tee.

Momma Tee, told me, "We should leave the world just a little better than we found it. Everything that we think, say, and do affects everyone else." These stories are Momma Tee's way and mine of making the world *just a little better.*

Enjoy these stories that Momma Tee told me to tell you.

[1] Beaudoin, Marie-Nathalie. *Responding to the Culture of Bullying & Disrespect.* Second Edition. Corwin Press, 2009, pps. xiv and 214.

Mike and Phoebe

This story grew out of my family's experience. Through the dedication and hard work of my uncle, Donald P. Stone, author of *The Fallen Prince,* we know that my great-grandmother's great-grandmother was kidnapped, stolen, and imprisoned on a ship that took people from Nigeria and Ethiopia and brought them to America, where they were sold as slaves. This story has been passed from family to family through the generations. My uncle Donald chronicled the lives of Mike and Phoebe and their posterity in *The Fallen Prince.* This story is dedicated to him.

◆ ◆ ◆

Momma Tee began telling this story around the time that she started blessing babies. This story is a part of our family's traditions; it is called for every Christmas and at all family reunions. It is woven into the tapestry of our family. I do not remember when I first heard this story. What I do know is that the story of Mike and Phoebe is my story. They are my legacy and I am their future. This story as much as about me as about them—it is a story for all times.

I loved it when our family gathered at Momma Tee's house. There were elders, young adults, and of course children, always children. Her house was not very large; it had only one bathroom and sometimes (especially in the summer) people spilled out onto the porch. Sitting on the steps were those family members wearing their "crowns" of silver or white passing around babies and catching those children who were just learning how to walk. There were always those young people who objected to being called "children" they sat furthest from their parents. It was always a full house.

We didn't mind. In fact we loved it, because those were "golden times." Momma Tee said, "If you are really lucky and if you recognize your blessings you will experience times in your life when the world turns golden. The air and space vibrates at a higher frequency until everything shimmers in a golden light. It is during these times when you know (beyond knowing)—that God is in Place, all is right with the Universe, and this is how we are meant to live." We shared food, laughter, music, family, and stories. Babies were held in laps, wiggly children settled; youth, young parents and elders gathered around Momma Tee like people who live in the Northern Hemisphere gather around the fire in winter. And, she began . . . ❧

Mike and Phoebe

*True love is a sacred trust
that moves us to open the door to possibility.*

—Momma Tee

Mike and Phoebe were bonds people, denied their freedom and called slaves. Phoebe's mother was taken from her country, her community, and her family—taken from all that she knew. Her hands were chained. Her feet were shackled. She was thrown into the dark belly of a ship with hundreds of other people where they laid head to toe, head to toe to endure a journey that I cannot imagine. Phoebe's mother was one of the hundreds of thousands of people stolen from their home country and brought to America—the land of the free—where they were sold into slavery.

Tall she was her skin almost ebony, the color reminiscent of freshly roasted coffee beans. She stood tall, erect, her body straight, and she moved with a grace, an elegance, and a peace that defied the circumstances that deprived her of her freedom. And they said that Phoebe was like her mother.

Mike was also tall, very tall. He stood head and shoulders above Phoebe. His skin was brown, his eyes a soft shade of sable with flecks of green and gold stood out against the chiseled features of his face. Mike's body was slim, wiry; hardened from many years of working in the fields.

Mike and Phoebe were married on Christmas morning in 1812. At that time, many people held in slavery omitted the words "till death do us part" from their marriage vows because slavery more often than death ripped families apart and scattered them throughout the country.

But Mike and Phoebe insisted—insisted—on including those words in their marriage vows. It was their commitment to stay together under any and all circumstances. It was a testament to the community, regardless of a system that denied them their freedom; they would remain together until parted by death. It was their promise of possibility in an impossible situation.

On that Christmas morning in that place, at that time holding hands and looking into each others eyes, they pledged to each other, "Till death do us part." It was the vow that they made to each other.

Mike and Phoebe were held as property by two different owners and lived on separate plantations, four miles apart. It did not matter if it was midsummer and the still air pushed the heat down long after the sun set. It did not matter if the earth was frozen and crunched under his steps. Each evening Mike walked. He walked after he worked from sun up to past sun down in the scorching heat. At the end of the day, when other bonds people were settling in for dinner or were kissing each other good night and were moving toward their straw mattresses, Mike walked—to his family. And when it was still dark before the sun rose and others were still in bed, turning, snuggling for just one more time, Mike began his morning walk, returning to his owners' plantation to work another day.

The early morning dew still hung in the air that spring morning as Mike stood at the beginning of that dusty South Carolina road. He stood and watched the train of wagons roll off on its westward journey.

The wheels of the wagons, the hooves of the oxen, cattle, and horses that pulled the wagons and the feet of the people that walked along side of those wagons raised dust. The dust swirled in the air and floated back to the earth. Dust fell on the bent heads and slumped shoulders of the bonds people as they walked alongside the wagons and it fell on Mike has he stood on the road and watched the train of wagons and his family head west.

When the dust had once again settled on the earth and Mike could no longer see the wagons or the people, he fell to his knees with a cry so desperate that it caused tears to flow down the hardened faces of the white overseers. Mike assailed the gods in heaven as his tears washed deep rivers in the dust on his face.

You see, Mike's wife, his pregnant wife Phoebe and their seven children were part of the procession heading west.

Phoebe's owner had decided to move his plantation from South Carolina to Alabama. So he had his furniture packed into wagons along with his pots, pans, and linens. He packed all his farming equipment and gathered his animals. And he gathered those people that he held in bondage and he moved them, too. He moved them without regard or consideration about what impact the move would have on their lives, on their families.

When Mike and Phoebe held each other that last night,

they renewed their pledge, their promise to one other, a vision that they held, to be together again as a family.

After a while (no one ever said how long) Mike pulled himself up from the ground. Brushing the dust off his pants and shirt, Mike went to see the man who held him in bondage.

That day in 1820 an agreement was made. Mike and his owner settled on a selling price, a selling price for a man of Mike's knowledge, capabilities, and character. They shook hands that morning, sealing the deal. The price they settled on that spring morning in 1820 was $1,900. On that morning, Phoebe's husband made another vow, a vow to his faraway family and to himself: he vowed to buy his freedom in four years. This was extraordinary, because the average length of time that it took a person to save enough money to buy their freedom was eight to ten years.

Ten to twelve hours each day, Mike labored in the fields. When the weather did not allow him and other bonds people to work in the fields, he built and reconstructed buildings on the plantation. He cared for the animals and he worked with the overseers, planning for the next crops. Mike received no wages for work as a slave; he was given breakfast each morning, strong black coffee and one or two biscuits or pieces of corn bread that were left over from the previous evening's meal.

At the end of the day the women made a hearty meal, "soul food" it was called, food made up of the parts of the pigs and the cattle that were normally thrown away or given to the dogs. The bondswomen included vegetables that they grew in the gardens around their lodgings. They made clothes from discarded grain sacks and scraps of material left over from the clothes they sewed for their owner's family. These meals and the clothing sustained Mike's health and kept him warm, but even the care of his fellow bonds people did not extinguish Mike's longing for his wife and children.

For Mike, the separation from his family was physically painful. He could find no peace, no place of comfort; he could not rest. He missed the long morning and evening walks. Those were the times when he prayed. It was in walking when he lived in gratitude for life, love, and the health of his family and loved ones. It was when he walked that Mike lived in possibility.

Because he could find no peace, he worked. In addition to the hours that Mike had to work as a slave, he found work. He worked during the times set aside for rest. He worked when others sat with their families for the evening meal. When others slept, Mike worked.

Bonds people were granted time off on Sundays to worship. Mike worked. When slaves were given Christmas and Easter free from working in the fields and other labor, Mike hired himself out as a skilled laborer. He worked as a blacksmith and as a carpenter. He was well known throughout the region and prized by other plantation owners for his knowledge of planting and crop rotation. Mike worked at whatever and wherever he could to earn money.

Because of circumstances beyond his control, it took Mike almost four and a half years, rather than the four years that he vowed it would take him, to earn enough money to purchase his freedom. In the early fall of 1825, he settled the final terms of his contract. Shaking hands with the man who had held him in bondage, Mike received the papers that he had earned—the papers that identified him as a free man. With vision, courage, commitment, and faith—faith in his vision, faith in himself, and faith in God—he had made the seemingly impossible, possible. He was a free man!

Mike had completed the first part of his vow. What was next? Now he had to travel over 300 miles from South Carolina to Alabama on foot to be with his family again.

On the road where four years earlier Mike had fallen down on his knees, he now stood. Standing where Phoebe and his seven children had walked away from him, Mike breathed in deeply, almost sniffing the air, he began walking.

He left late in the evening, that time just before the moon rose. With his head held high and his back straight, that late fall evening, Mike began his journey west. To avoid capture, he traveled late at night and early in the morning. To hide from bounty hunters he walked along remote waterways and through the thickly wooded forests. As he walked, instinctively he followed the moon. The nights were cool, almost cold, but they were clear. He traveled until the sun turned the dawn warm. When the sweat began to pool in the crevice of his throat, he looked for a place to sleep.

He sometimes traveled on roads teeming with slave traders and bounty hunters with only a piece of paper declaring him a freeman, a paper that someone could snatch away from him at any moment—and he could once again be held in bondage.

He relied on the moon and the stars to guide his journey. A journey that took that long-ago wagon train three weeks took Mike just five days.

When he reached Montgomery, Alabama, Mike was told that Snow Hill was 60 miles due West, a two-day walk. He could not begin his journey immediately, however. Town officials, who did not believe that he was a free man, held him for three days. Finally, when the sun was just cresting the horizon, Mike set off again, walking.

Day approached dusk when Mike arrived at the plantation called Snow Hill. On both sides of the road, he saw people working in the field. The sun was almost down and people still worked. Seeing Mike, the field workers began to call to him, "Mike? Mike, is that you? Aren't you Phoebe's husband?" He waved at the familiar faces, but he did not stop. Shouting across the field, he asked the location of the well and of the big house.

Like a wind whipped wildfire crossing dry plains, word spread through the plantation. "Mike's here," people shouted. "Mike! Phoebe's husband, here, now, in this time and at this place he is here and he is a free man."

At the well, Mike splashed water on his head and shoulders. Water ran down his face and neck, washing away the dirt from the road. After shaking the water out of his hair and putting on his only other shirt, he walked through the thin woods and up a short rise to the big house. Knocking at the back door, he requested an audience with Phoebe's owner. The owner of his wife and children was a paunchy man with red cheeks and a bulbous rose colored nose. He met with Mike in his library. Phoebe's owner already knew about Mike's skills, talents, and he knew Mike to be a man of strong character, one who was true to his word. He hired Mike that day as a freeman, to work on his plantation.

To seal their agreement, they shook hands. That day, Mike left the big house by the front door. When he stepped out onto the porch, as far as he could see he saw faces: black, brown, tan and almond faces. Some people were still running, others shouting and calling his name, and many were crying tears of joy, tears of witnessing what many felt—the impossible made possible.

At first he did not see her, there were so many people but as the crowd pushed Phoebe forward, they pushed Mike off the porch; husband and wife fell into each other's arms.

They held on to each other as though they would never let the other go. It took their children—their children eager for their father—to pull them apart. Mike held up each one of his children, kissing their faces, swinging them around and laughing, until he came to the last, the youngest, the one that he had never seen. He held that one up to the heavens, it was then that Mike fell to the earth on his knees in gratitude. The pain that Mike carried for those four plus years left him, he was home.

That night Mike and Phoebe did not sleep. They laid in each other arms, touching, kissing, squeezing, holding each other, and laughing. They could not quite believe that it was true, that they were together. As the sun rose bringing a new day, as they gave thanks and they remembered an ancient African blessing; a blessing whispered in the ears of newly born babies.

Life is whatever you want it to be. The choice is yours.
You can be whatever you want to be
and do whatever you choose to do.
You are spirit.

Mike and Phoebe were reunited in 1825. They had three more children for a total of eleven. They continued their lives together for almost 40 years.

Together, they lived to see the outbreak of the War Between the States, but they died before it was concluded. Mike went home in 1863 and Phoebe followed her husband in 1864. They did not live to see the end of slavery, but each one of their eleven children would see, smell, feel, and taste the full fruits of freedom. Their children stood witness to the strength, courage, commitment, and vision of those who preceded them. They stood witness to the fact that the impossible was made possible, their lives a living testament to their parents' love.

◆ ◆ ◆

Momma Tee has told this story countless times. Some say it is a story of courage and strength, others say it is a story about determination and tenacity. There are those who call it a story about commitment and faith. Once someone said, "That Mike was a stubborn man."

Tee would smile and nod her head, "Yes," she said, "this story is all of that, but truly, truly this is a love story."

Bubble Trouble

Bubbles! Momma Tee blew bubbles! She blew bubbles at births and baptisms. She blew bubbles at birthday parties and on special occasions. She blew bubbles at graduations and at weddings. And she blew bubbles at wakes and funerals.

There are some who said, "She's crazy!"

Momma Tee said, "Bubbles are little bits of magic here on earth. Just blow a few bubbles and watch people change. Children become giddy and begin to jump, dance and laugh and adults become children. Bubbles, these captured bits of air shimmer, glisten, and sparkle in a rainbow of colors and they make people think of magic and fantasy."

Bubbles filled with the breath of love welcome newly born babies. Capturing the baby's attention for just a moment, then they burst, baptizing the baby with droplets of love.

Bubbles delight everyone. They bring joy, fantasy, magic, color, and laughter to parties. Bubbles surround a newly married couple with love and remind the graduate of childhood, adulthood, and a bright new future where anything is possible.

Bubbles at funerals and wakes are messages of love that accompany our dear ones home.

And, sometimes Momma Tee just sat on her porch, blowing bubbles.

One day Momma Tee was sitting on the porch blowing bubbles and she called to the children, "Children!"

They arrived in a cloud of bubbles.

Pointing to the bubbles she asked them, "What do you think these are?" The movement of her hand stirred the air causing the bubbles to spin, turn, and dance.

"Bubbles, Momma Tee," they answered almost in chorus each one trying to catch one of the shining, glistening orbs, "just bubbles."

Looking at them she asked, "Did you know that you can turn nothing into something, just by thinking it? Did you know you can turn a bubble into a whole mess of trouble just by using your mind? I know a story about turning nothing into something and how a powerful warrior king learned a very important lesson from a little girl."

The children gathered around her, sitting here, there, everywhere on the porch. As they sat, a hush settled upon each one. They sat; some sat straight-backed, eyes open and hands in their laps. Others sat crossed-legged elbows on knees, head in hands, and their eyes on Momma Tee. Some stretched on their back, knees raise, eyes closed, their head resting in the pillow of their arms. It was in that hush that she began. ֍

The Story
Bubble Trouble

*You can turn nothing into something
just by using your mind.
You can turn a bubble into a whole lot of trouble.*
—**Momma Tee**

It happened a long, long time ago, when Africa was young and ruled by powerful warrior kings.

King Akbari was the most powerful king of them all. It was said that his kingdom had so many villages and his land so vast that if you stood on the highest point in Akbari's kingdom and looked in all four directions as far as you could see, until the earth curved, you still could not see all of his kingdom. He lived on the continent of Africa on the northwest coast in a little village called Uzama.

Early each morning, Akbari and his warriors would ride through the village of Uzama to make sure that all was safe and free from intrusion.

One particular morning, when Akbari and his warriors were coming back from their morning ride, as they approached the village they saw on the riverbank sparkling, shining, and shimmering in a rainbow of colors in the early morning sun was a big, no it was huge, no, no it was gigantic . . . it was a gigantic bubble.

King Akbari and his warriors stopped. The King looked at the bubble, he looked at his warriors, and he looked back at the bubble. Akbari's warriors looked at their king and they looked at the bubble. Together they all turned as one and looked back at their king.

Akbari jumped down from his horse, carrying his royal spear he ran toward the bubble. The king stopped a royal distance from the bubble, he pointed his royal spear at the gigantic bubble and declared, "THIS IS BIG TROUBLE!"

Bubble Trouble, Trouble Bubble
Everybody knows that a gigantic bubble
shining and shimmering
in a rainbow of colors
in the early morning sun is nothing but
BIG TROUBLE!

In his loudest voice, the King declared, "I, Akbari, the most powerful king in all of Africa will get rid of this big trouble right now."

Mounting his horse and holding his royal spear high, Akbari rode down the riverbank. He set off, riding swift like the winter's North wind, Akbari charged the bubble. His royal spear hit the bubble and bounced off. King Akbari lost his balance and he tumbled head first, landing right into the middle of the gigantic bubble.

Bubble Trouble, Trouble Bubble
Everybody knows that this is big trouble
Because a king cannot rule
A kingdom from inside a Bubble!

Surprised and perhaps a little stunned, Akbari pushed on the inside wall of the bubble, and he could not get out. He used his fists, head, shoulders, and feet. He could not break out of the bubble. Near exhaustion, the king called for his Red Warrior. His Red Warrior came forward. The warrior was dressed entirely in red from the top of his head to the tip of his toes. Bowing low, he greeted his king asking, "My king, how may I serve you?"

Akbari shouted, "Get me out of this trouble!"

The Red Warrior stepped back and looked at the bubble and looked at his king and he said, "My king, I am afraid that I will hurt you."

Between clenched teeth Akbari shouted, "I will be OK, just get me out of this big trouble."

Backing away, the Red warrior said, "As you wish."

The Red warrior mounted his red horse, and with his sword in hand he rode down the riverbank. As pointed and as powerful as a bolt of lighting with his red locks flying in the wind, the Red warrior charged the bubble. The Red Warrior's sword hit the bubble and bounced off and King Akbari was still in the middle of the bubble.

Bubble Trouble, Trouble Bubble
Everybody knows that this is big trouble
Because a king cannot rule
A kingdom from inside a Bubble!

Akbari was even more furious. He pressed his face so hard against the bubble that he flattened his nose. With his face distorted, pushing the inside of the bubble with his hands, Akbari called for his Blue Warrior. The Blue Warrior came forward. He was dressed entirely in blue from the top of his head to the tip of his toes. Bowing low, he greeted his king asking, "My king, how may I serve you?"

With his face still pressed up against the inside wall of the bubble, Akbari screamed between clinched teeth, "Get me out of this trouble!"

The Blue Warrior stepped back, looked at the bubble and looked at his king, and he said, 'My king, I am afraid I will hurt you."

Akbari shouted. "I will be OK, just get me out of this big trouble."

Backing away, the Blue warrior said, "As you wish."

The Blue Warrior pulled out his short knife and he jogged down the riverbank. Running faster than an arrow shot from a bow, his blue locks flying in the wind, the Blue Warrior charged the bubble. His knife hit the bubble and bounced off and King Akbari was still inside the bubble.

Bubble Trouble, Trouble Bubble
Everybody knows that this is big trouble
Because a king cannot rule
A kingdom from inside a Bubble!

The sun was high in the sky and the day was getting hot. The bubble was surrounded by knives, spears, machetes, swords, and rocks of every size and shape. Akbari's men sat on the ground around the bubble scratching their heads.

And, King Akbari, still in the middle of the bubble trouble, sat with this head in his hands.

At that moment, from the direction of the village, children's voices could be heard. It was the village children coming to the river for their daily swim.

As the children rounded the bend and saw the bubble they stopped. Their mouths dropped open, and their eyes grew big. They said, "What a big bubble! It's beautiful! Look at all of the colors. I've never seen a bubble that big. It's the biggest bubble I've ever seen! Oh my, what a big, beautiful bubble!" Then from the very back of the group of children, a little girl said, "That's my daddy in the middle of that gigantic bubble."

Hearing the children's voices, Akbari jumped to his feet. Standing in the middle of the bubble he called to his men shouting, "Warriors, stop the children! Keep them away from this bubble trouble."

Akbari's warriors ran toward the children to keep them from the trouble. The children, thinking it was a game, began to laugh. They ran, hopped, skipped, jumped, and danced away from the warriors.

Everyone knows that little African girls are very smart. Everyone also knows that little African girls can out run, out hop, out skip, out jump, and out dance any old warrior, any day.

Akbari's daughter, like most little African girls, was very smart and very quick on her feet. So she ran, hopped, skipped, jumped, and danced around all the warriors until she stood before the bubble and her father. Akbari's daughter looked at the bubble and she looked at her father. She looked at her father and she looked at the bubble. Then she asked "Daddy, what are you doing in the middle of that bubble?"

King Akbari said, "Daughter, stay away, stay away! Stay away from this bubble trouble."

But before he could finish, his daughter, bending forward, with two fingers pinched the bubble, *and poof*, the bubble was gone. Surprised, Akbari looked at his daughter.

The king's daughter said, "Daddy, if you treat it like a bubble, it will act like a bubble."

Bubble Trouble, Trouble Bubble
Everybody knows that you can turn nothing into something
just by using your mind.
You can turn a bubble into a whole lot of trouble or
you can treat it like a bubble.

The Legend of Susie Edwards

"Child, it's time!" Momma Tee called to me from the bedroom. "Child, the Story Bowl is 'bout to run over, it's time."

Quickly throwing my bath towel over the rod, I ran to bed. Still damp from my bath, I snuggled under crisp, fragrant, sun-dried sheets. Tucking the covers around my body, legs, and feet, tickling my neck and arms, Momma Tee smothered me with warm kisses.

Finally, when we were both breathless, her eyes sparkling and filled with mirth, she reached for the Story Bowl.

The Story Bowl is older than old. Momma Tee said that it was carried over on a ship that transported people who had been kidnapped from Africa and brought to America where they were sold as slaves. The Story Bowl traveled hidden in the skirts and head wraps of the stolen women. The Story Bowl is a gourd the size of a large honeydew melon cut in half. The whole universe is in the Story Bowl, the top half represents the heavens with the stars, sun, moon, and galaxies and the bottom half the earth, the oceans and all the animals, birds and men that walked on its surface and flew in the skies. When the two halves of the Story Bowl are joined together, the matching lips become the horizon joining the heavens and the earth. The colors of the patterned animals, symbols, and people on the surface of the bowl have long faded, worn away by the many hands and the passage of time.

The Story Bowl has been in our family longer than our memories. It has been handed down from grandmother to granddaughter for generations. The Story Bowl holds our family's stories. I've learned who I am through the courage, losses, strengths, loves, and accomplishments of my foremothers.

Tonight, like so many nights before, snuggled close to Momma Tee, magic happens, she opens the universe and stories pour out. ❧

The Legend of Susie Edwards

All legends grow out of a seed of truth.
The legend of Susie Edwards is such a legend.
A legend clothed in mystery and in faith.

—Momma Tee

At the turn of the century, when many Blacks were struggling to go beyond the reach of slavery, William James Edwards, a colleague of Booker T. Washington, established Snow Hill Normal and Industrial Institute for Black Americans. Snow Hill Institute of Technology was an industrial, agricultural and teachers college established in 1890, opening its doors in 1894. A testament to his grandparents, Mike and Phoebe, William Edwards overcame enormous obstacles to become one who marks a great age in the history of the African American people.

Susie Edwards, the wife of William J. Edwards the founder and principal of the Snow Hill Institute, worked alongside her husband. Together, with commitment, courage, and faith, they made their vision possible.

We called our great grandfather, Poppa and his wife Susie, my greatgrandmother we called Momma Susie.

Momma Susie was my maternal great grandmother. She and Poppa lived in a small village 60 miles due west of Montgomery, Alabama in Wilcox County, called Snow

Hill. Susie Edwards, a petite, slight, brown skinned woman standing no more than five tall, is the bravest woman that I know. She told me this story of the impossible becoming possible.

While the Snow Hill Institute flourished serving people of African Heritage from all across the country many local whites became bitter and angry because Black Americans who started as slaves or sons and daughters of slaves were learning skills and receiving an education that far exceeded their own. The school was located on a small hill, on prized, fertile land surrounded by Mississippi Pines. The house that Poppa and Momma lived in sat on a rise to the left of the school.

Ruling whites in Wilcox County approached William Edwards, Poppa, time after time to persuade, coerce, and try to frighten him into selling his land to them. Poppa steadfastly refused. He declared that Snow Hill Institute belonged to him and his family for the benefit of Black Americans everywhere. Poppa would not sell! He could not be swayed by money or by fear.

In order to raise money for the school, Poppa traveled throughout the south and to the north, lecturing and singing. When Poppa was away on one of these trips, Momma Susie was visited by cloaked phantoms.

◆ ◆ ◆

It was a hot summer night—calm, clear, and still. School was not in session, so there was no one on campus. It was the darkest time of the night, the time just before the moon rose. The time when the night creatures could be heard practicing for their nightly concert of music to pay homage to the rising moon!

At first, Momma Susie said that she thought that it was thunder. But the persistence of the sound made her aware that it was not. Going to her front window, she parted the curtains and looked out. She saw what looked like ghosts. It was then that she knew that the demons had been unleashed from hell.

Mounted on reluctant horses, white sheets whipping and slashing the night, carrying balls of fire held in torches to light their way, the Ku Klux Klan stormed the campus.

They drove their horses up the hill and onto the campus. Using their horses and voices as battering rams, the Klan burst through the hardwood doors of the school and pushed their horses onto the school's stately halls.

The air filled with a mad rhythm, played by the pounding of the horse's hooves on the schools wooden floors. The phantoms pounded walls, broke doors, smashed desks, and destroyed precious books. Mad they were, screaming obscenities and throwing foul words into the silent dignified building. These creatures spit out their rage, their bitterness, their anger and their feelings of being small and powerless against the silent walls. Then, all at once, as if gaining courage from the silence, the demons poured out the doors and swarmed down the hill, surrounding Poppa's house and within it my great grandmother, Susie Edwards.

Everywhere she looked, from every window Susie Edwards saw fire—red, yellow, and blue flames dancing against the black of the night. Surrounded by fire she said, "They appeared as spirits, ghosts floating on the dark of the night."

Garbled, muffled voices called her. They spat at her, calling her repulsive, filthy names. Names used by those who mean to demean, degrade, and step on others so that they could feel whole. Their screaming voices filled the air. They called her that repugnant name, that word that tears at the soul, that vile name whose only purpose was to denigrate. They called to her.

"N..., get out here! Get out here now you black b... Come out now! Get out here or we will burn you and your house to the ground." My great grandmother, holding her head high, walked from the light that filled her home out onto the porch and into the darkness surrounding her house.

Sitting low in his saddle, hiding under an ill-fitting, dirty, tattered sheet, a single phantom coerced his horse to the foot of the porch.

Shoving a wrinkled, dirty paper in her face, he screamed at her, "Sign this!"

The paper was a deed to the College, Poppa and Momma's house, and all of its surrounding land and buildings.

A chorus of mad, hysterical voices filled the air.

Momma Susie stood on the porch and stared and into the circle of fire. Slowly, once, only once did she shake her head, "No!" She refused to speak to these cowards who came in the dead of night when she was alone; these bullies who would not even show their faces as they threatened her life.

Momma Susie refused to look at the paper. She refused to sign. She refused to be moved by their camouflage, she refused to give into fear.

The legend said time stood still, the night went silent. Everything hung, as if waiting for a cue. Even the night animals were quiet and the wind dared not move.

Susie Edwards stood on her porch.

Suddenly, the hooded man at the foot of the stairs screamed. His horse shrieked, reared back, and dumped him to the ground. The frightened horse backed away from the porch, turned, and fled into the night. The man's hood fell away, exposing him alone. His torch went out as it fell to the ground returning him to darkness.

Legend says that his cry piercing the night was heard miles away.

The shrieks of horses grew louder only to be drowned out by the terrified screams of the hooded men.

The circle of fire fell apart.

Shedding the rest of his sheet, the unmasked man at the foot of the porch ran into the night. Running until he was plucked from the ground by a fleeing crony. Holding on to each other, their eyes wide, their mouths open, they fled. The band of not so brave men, in not so white sheets fled, returning to the hell from which they had sprung.

And, once again, it was a hot summer night in Alabama, clear, calm, and still. The moon brightly shone, stars opened their eye, and the night creatures sang in full chorus.

Momma Susie stood on her front porch, starring in the direction where the apparitions had disappeared.

She was often asked, "What did you do? Why did they leave? What happened?"

Momma Susie answered, "I do not know why they left. I stood on my porch that night and prayed."

She said, "I closed my eyes and prayed to the One God. I called the names of African attributes, Obatala for strength and Oya for courage. I asked Jesus for protection and I remembered those who came before me.

She told me that she drew strength from the memory of her great grandmother, Phoebe's mother, who was stolen, kidnapped from her family in Africa, to endure an unimaginable journey across the waters to America where she was sold as a slave. And yet, she moved with a grace, dignity, and a peace that belied the circumstances that denied her freedom, a peace that could not be taken from her. Impossible?

She drew courage from Mike and Phoebe, her grandparents who were held in bondage and called slaves. Separated when Phoebe's owner moved his plantation across states, against all odds they were reunited and remained together until parted by death. Impossible? Possible!

She remembered her husband who established a college in a community in rural Alabama. A vision, grounded in faith, built on commitment and courage became a reality. The impossible made possible. Momma Susie, remembering the triumphs of her foremothers and forefathers, prayed for the impossible to be possible.

Susie Edwards said of that night, "I remember hearing the cries and screams of men, shrieks of horses, and the thundering of the horse's hoofs diminishing in retreat. I opened my eyes and saw the lights of their torches in the distance going out one by one like someone walking through the house turning off the lights until the night was again dark. It was then that I first felt the pain in my head. I raised my hand to my head here, just above my brow and found a lump the size of a walnut."

◆ ◆ ◆

The legend said she grew. Some said she was some sort of witch; they called her a voodoo priestess. The legend said, "The cloaked men saw her lips moving but did not hear a word." A sorceress, a demon from hell others told because that night she became a giant. The white people in the area swore on the Bible that she stood on the front porch that night and grew. They whispered that she grew until she towered over their hooded crony at the foot of her porch. She grew until the cloaked men encircling her house were dwarfed. She grew until her head hit the top of the porch and still she grew. Those who would admit that they were there and those who passed on the legend said, "She became enormous, gigantic, standing witness to their actions."

The Black ministers said, "Susie Edwards stood witness to their inhumanity reflecting it back until they became terrified of themselves."

At the end, people said that Momma Susie chuckled under her breath, "After that night the white people never bothered us again."

Momma Susie said, "I sat watch on my porch through the night and as the dawn broke, bringing a new day I remembered my grandmother and the whispered blessing:"

"Be strong!
Use your inner sight—see what is really, real.
Be not swayed from your path,
Remain true to yourself and remember.
You are Spirit."

"Remember," Momma Tee whispered in my ear,

"remember."

The Man Who
Moved a Mountain

A Man Who Moved a Mountain is a story about the journey of an ordinary boy who over the course of a lifetime transforms an extraordinary vision into an extraordinary reality. He finds faith in the face of massive doubt, musters resilience to overcome near-fatal challenges, and discovers inner courage and strength that even he, at times, does not know he possesses. He moves a mountain much like those many of us wish would get out of our way. ❧

The Story
A Man Who Moved a Mountain

Are there ever times when you feel that a "mountain"
stands in the way of your getting ahead?
And, might you have wondered,
"If I could only move that mountain...."

—Momma Tee

In ancient times, when the earth was new, thousands of years before there were great machines that moved earth, before there were cars and freeways, before even great ships crossed the high seas and engines pulled boxes on tracks. Even before people rode two wheel cycles, in a place that was then called the Orient, lived a man who moved a mountain.

Nestled between two mountains lay a fertile valley, and in this valley lived a farmer. He really was a gardener, because he grew and sold flowers. He grew red, blue, pink, purple, orange, and yellow flowers. He grew flowers that bloomed in the spring and in the fall. He grew flowers that brought sunshine in the winters and flowers that blew cool breezes in the summer. He owned a large plot of land, but he was only able to grow flowers on a small portion of his land because most of it lay in the shadow cast by one of the mountains.

Frequently the gardener would look up at the mountain and say, "If only I could move that mountain, I could grow more flowers."

One sunny day while working in the garden with his young son, the man said, "If only I could move that mountain, I could grow more flowers."

The gardener's son said, "Father, why don't you move the mountain." The gardener with eyes full of love, looked at his son and replied, "Son, I cannot move a mountain. I am only a man."

That evening, the gardener's son, who was not yet 12 years old, walked to the top of the mountain. He looked out between the two mountains at the valley below and he saw that it formed the pattern of a patchwork quilt made up of the farms, gardens, roads, and the houses of the people who lived in the valley. Running along the north side of the valley was a river.

He looked for his father's farm. He saw that much of his father's land lay in the shadow of the mountain, and then he turned and looked out over the other side. He saw the marsh. The ground was wet and soggy. He could see that the river that ran through the valley overran its banks and much of the year the ground lay wet, under water.

The gardener's son stood for a long time looking out quietly over the valley and back over at the marsh. After a while, he walked down the mountain. He went to this father's shed where the gardening tools were kept. The boy searched until he found two buckets. Then he walked back up the mountain carrying the two buckets. When he got to the top of the mountain, he filled his two buckets with earth and walked back down.

Every day the young boy walked up the mountain, filled

two buckets with earth, and walked back down. Twelve full moons passed when his father finally asked, "Son, what are you doing? Each day you take two buckets, walk to the top of the mountain, fill them with earth and walk back down. What are you doing? Why are you doing this?

The young boy replied, "Father, I am moving the mountain."

Shaking his head, the gardener said, "Son, you are only a boy. You cannot move a mountain."

The boy, with his eyes full of love, looked at father and said, "Father, I can see it. I will move that mountain. I will move the mountain so that you can grow more flowers."

Time passes as it does and every day the gardener's son got up in the morning, ate breakfast, played with his friends, studied the sacred scrolls and took the two buckets, walked up the mountain, filled them with earth, and walked back down.

And the boy grew into a young man.

Life in the valley was not always easy. There were times when the rains did not come when they should or the rains fell too heavily and the valley flooded. Flying insects the size of birds came one year and ate all the rice. That year, many people died. Because life in the valley was so hard, many young people left the valley seeking work and an easier life over the mountain. The gardener's son did not leave. He stayed in the valley between the mountains and worked with his father in the garden. And every day he took two buckets, walked up the mountain, filled them with earth, and walked back down.

People in the village began to talk about the young man. They said that he was a good person, that he grew beautiful flowers, that he gave a good product for a fair price, and that he gave back to his community. But, they said that he was not quite right in the head. Many thought that he was a little crazy, because every day he took two buckets, walked up the mountain, filled the buckets with earth, and walked back down. They said that it was not normal for man to think that he could move a mountain.

There was a young woman in the village who watched the young man. She liked the way he looked. She admired his character, but she did not understand why it was that every day that he took two buckets, walked up the mountain, filled them with earth, and walked back down. One day, she secretly followed him as he walked up the mountain carrying the two buckets. She watched as he filled the buckets with earth and she followed him when he walked down. When he neared his father's home, she stopped him and asked, "Why is it that every day you take two buckets, walk up the mountain, fill them with earth, and walk back down?"

The young man stopped. He turned over one of the buckets, and, brushing off the loose dirt, he invited the young woman to sit. He turned over the other bucket and sat down, too. The man's soft quiet voice outlined a picture that only he had seen. With his words and heart he colored in the spaces and created a vision for her to see.

They began to see each other. Soon they fell in love and very soon after they agreed to be married.

The cherry blossoms colored the trees pink and white the day of their wedding. On the morning that he was to be married, the young man got up before the sun rose. He took his two buckets, walked up the mountain, filled them with earth, and walked back down. That day, the day that he would marry his bride, the young man went up the mountain again and filled two more buckets with earth and walked back down.

There was a great marriage ceremony, filled with flowers, friends, laughter, love and dreams—dreams of the impossible becoming possible.

Before the winter's snow fell that year, the old gardener died.

Planting flowers on his father's final earthly resting place, the young man, with tears still wet on his checks, whispered, "Father, I will move the mountain!"

Then the young man walked to what was now his shed where the gardening tools were kept. He took two buckets, walked up the mountain, filled them with earth, and walked back down. That day, the young man went up the mountain again and filled two more buckets with earth and walked back down.

There were times when the young man did not feel like walking up the mountain, especially in the winter, when the cold wind cut like a knife's sharp edge and the skies dripped ice. The young man would wake up, look out the window and sigh. Sitting on the edge of his bed, he pulled on leggings, put on two pairs of socks (sometimes he would even put on two coats), his gloves, and his hat. Wrapping a long woolen scarf around his neck and mouth, he picked up the two buckets and walked up the mountain. At the top, he filled the two buckets with frozen or wet earth, and then he walked back down. Sometimes his steps were slow.

But, if you were watching, you would notice that his steps were lighter when he came back down the mountain. And if you listened carefully, you would even hear him humming or singing. His steps coming down the mountain, even when he was carrying two buckets full of wet, frozen earth were always sprightlier.

Time passes as it does and man and his wife had a child. On the morning that their child was born, the man sat with his wife, holding her hand and filling her mind's eye with a vision. When their son was born, the man held his brand new baby in his arms.

Father and son looked into each other's eyes. Anyone looking at them knew it was love. The man held his son, staring into his eyes until his wife, eager for her son, convinced her husband to let her hold their baby.

Later that morning, the man walked to his shed and took his two buckets, walked up the mountain, filled them with earth, and walked back down. That day, the day his son was born, the man went back up the mountain and filled two more buckets with earth and walked back down.

In the blink of an eye, the man's son was walking. On warm days, you could see him walking with his father. He would often take two little cups as he walked with his father up the mountain. At the top, he would fill his two cups with earth and walk with his father back down the mountain.

In a turn of a head, the boy was old enough to go to school. In school, he began to hear children on the play yard whisper, "That's the son of the crazy man who goes up the mountain every day."

When he went to the market with his mother, he heard women whisper over the vegetables and behind the fruit. Pointing to him and his mother and shaking their heads, the women whispered, "That poor woman. That poor child does not have a chance with a crazy man for his father."

And he watched the old men in the park, peering over their board games, glancing at him shaking their heads. They said, "It is too sad, too sad. No one in their right mind would walk, every day, to the top of the mountain, fill two buckets with earth and walk back down. He thinks he is more than human. It is too sad, too sad."

Running home, he called to his father and shouted, "Father, father you must stop going up the mountain. Everyone is talking about you. You must stop."

The man took his son's hand and led him to the garden. He sat with him pointing to the mountain. His soft quiet voice painted a picture and his words colored in the spaces until his son too could see his vision. But the man's son said, "Father yes, I see it but everyone says that it cannot be done! They say that you are crazy."

Still holding his son's hand in his, the man looked deeply into his eyes and replied, "Son, it is not an easy thing to move a mountain." Then the man walked out to his shed, took his two buckets, walked up the mountain, filled the buckets with earth, and walked back down.

The son stood for a while, watching his father. With his eyes filled with tears, he turned, went into the house, and closed the door. The man's son never again went up the mountain with his father.

When the man's son grew old enough, not wanting to work in the garden of the man some called crazy, he left the valley. He went over the mountain to the big city to seek work. He stayed in the big city, far from the valley, far from his father's garden, and far from the mountain.

The man's son spent more that 20-harvest seasons in the city, when he received message saying that his father was very sick. The message said that he should come home.

The son returned home to find his father in bed. The village doctor was sitting with him. The man was surprised to see that his father was an old man. His frail, wilted body barely made a bump in the bed covers. At the foot of his father's bed were two tattered, dirty buckets.

Taking the son aside, the doctor told the man's son that his father would live longer if he did not go up the mountain every day.

Falling to his knees next to this father's bed, he pleaded, "Father, why don't you stop? The doctor says that you would live longer if only you would stop going up the mountain every day."

The father and son looked into each other's eyes. Anyone looking at them knew it was love.

Taking his son's hands the old man said, "Son, it is not an easy thing to move a mountain."

That night before the old man closed his eyes, still holding his son's hand, he asked his son to lean close. His son kneeling next to his father's bed lowered his head until his father's lips almost touched his ear. It was then that the old man whispered, "Son, if you believe you can move a mountain, if you can see it, if you stay committed, if you have courage, and if you have faith you can make the impossible possible, you can move a mountain." The son felt the warm dry lips of his father kiss him gently, lovingly on his cheek. With that the old gardener closed his eyes and did not open them again in this world.

At the old man's "home going celebration" the temple overflowed with people. People stood on the porch and on the steps. They lined the walkways and still more people from the valley came. People walked long distances and stood in long lines to enter the temple to pay their respect to the old man who, every day, walked up the mountain, filled two buckets with earth, and walked back down.

The people told the man's son that his father was an honorable man, that he was a good person who he grew beautiful flowers, that he gave a good product for a fair price, and that he always worked in his community. Old women stopped him. They told him stories of how his father would always give them flowers to lay on their husband's grave. Men told the story about the last great flood and how his father had taken in two families until their lands dried out and their homes could be rebuilt. He heard story after story about his father. His father was a man of good character who had earned the respect, admiration, and love of everyone in the village. The old priest, the baker, and his school chums stopped him and apologized to him for their whispers of long ago. Hanging their heads and dropping their eyes, they told him how it had just taken them a little longer to see his father's vision.

After his father was laid to rest, the man's son went to his father's garden. He stood in the garden appreciating the flowers that were the result of his father's hard work.

As he stood, he noticed that a portion of his father's land where flowers never grew when he was a boy was now in bloom. The garden was filled with red, yellow, blue, pink, and white flowers. The yellow and orange flowers gently moved, stirred by the wind. The garden was a celebration of flowers, flowers in the wind bowing to the earth. They bloomed everywhere. Stunned, he could see that the sun shone in his father's garden.

Raising his hands to shade his eyes from the sun's brilliance, he turned and looked up at the mountain. At first he wasn't sure. At first he thought he was tired from the day and that he was not focusing clearly. Blinking his eyes again, it looked like a portion of the mountain had been moved.

He went quickly to the foot of the mountain, looked up, and began to walk. At the top of the mountain he looked out. He saw that the valley below formed the pattern of a patchwork quilt made up of the farms, gardens, roads, and houses of the people who lived in the valley. Running along the north side of the valley was a river. He looked and found his father's garden and the land that once lay in the shadow of the mountain, the place where flowers could not grow when he was a child, was now a chorus of flowers singing praises to the sun.

Then he turned and looked on the other side of the mountain to the place that had been wet, a marsh. Where the river once overflowed its banks was now built up, so that the river ran within its banks. And where water once stood, flowers now waved at him in the breeze.

The man's son stood for a long time at the top of the mountain, looking from side to side. He went into his father's house, picked up the two tattered, dirty buckets from the foot of his father's bed, and walked up the mountain, filled the two buckets with earth, and walked back down.

The man's son stayed in the village between the two mountains.

The next day when the old man's son walked on the road that led to the mountain, he saw other people from the village walking up the mountain. They were all carrying buckets or pails of all sizes and shapes. Some of the young men carried two, three, and sometimes four buckets as if to prove their manhood. The men mostly carried two buckets, the women and girls carried whatever was comfortable, and the young children carried cups with small spoons.

The man who went to the top of the mountain every day had taught the people in the village that it is not an easy thing to move a mountain. But if you have vision, if you are committed, if you have the courage to stand up for what you believe in, and if you have faith, you too can move a mountain.

A Legacy
My Chat with a Nazi

This story grew out of an experience when two people dared to live in possibility. The story of how these two people were drawn to each other traces back to the beginning of time, when the universe aligned itself to this possibility. The choice they made sent vibrations into the universe that will affect human kind until the end of time. This is a story of how two souls dared to surrender to the unknown to accept the possibility of peace, the possibility of love.

As in the stories of old that have been told throughout time, understanding comes from the willingness to surrender to the unknown.

Many times, walking into possibility takes vision, but it always takes courage and commitment. And it would be impossible, absolutely impossible without faith.

There are some who could testify to the veracity of my words. There will be those who will say this and others and who will say that. I can't testify to the veracity of their words. I can only tell my story, my truth.

After hearing this story, a friend challenged me: "Tell the story, and write it down. It's your story, tell it!" Another wanted to know if the Nazi and I had been intimate: "Did your relationship become sexual?" My darling sister told me time and time again, "Do what you do best, tell the story!" So I am doing what I do best—telling the story!

This story came back to me during the 2008 presidential election, when someone chided, even mocked one of the presidential nominees, laughing and asking "How can the President, sit down and talk to those whose intention is to do us harm?" It was then that this story flew back to my mind. It was then that I wrote this down. I share this with you now as a possibility!

This story is a gift, a gift from the universe of two people who chose to walk together into possibility. ॐ

The Story
A Legacy
My Chat with a Nazi

It's amazing the stories that we tell ourselves,
the stories that we choose to believe.
It is those stories that we choose to believe
that become our life

—Momma Tee

She stood in a room full of people at the club, with a plastic glass of tepid, sour wine in her hands, alone. The first smell of the wine told her that she did not want to drink it, but she held on to the glass; she had to have something to hold on to. It was a party and she was not in a party mood. She stood with her back against the wall, people-watching and wishing that they had some good red wine, wishing that she was somewhere, almost anywhere else.

This story begins in the early 1980's. She was married in 1983, separated in 1988, and divorced in 1992. She and her former husband lived in madness for two years before she had had enough and asked him to leave her house. This story tells of a meeting set in place at the beginning of time. It was a time of change. It was time for her to let go of what she had hoped for, what she believed in, and what she had expected. It was time for her step into the unknown. She knew change was coming; she could feel it taking shape in her mind, unfolding her heart, and moving throughout her body. It was a time for change. Yet, still she resisted, holding onto the familiar pain until resisting became too painful, until she fell on her knees crying out to the Universe, sobbing to God, "I surrender, Thy will not mine!" She had a choice to die or to live. She chose life. She chose to surrender to the unknown, and that was when she stepped into possibility.

◆ ◆ ◆

It was winter 1986; she had not seen her husband in four days.

This time she was not freaking out. She knew he was off somewhere, with someone, and, like always, he would come back. The first time he disappeared she did freak. She had called everyone—his best friend, his job, his mother, his sister, the police, and she even asked his dog if he knew where he was. She called his work dozens of times, so worried was she that she could not sleep or eat. She could not imagine that he would stay away without telling her. She worried, she cried, and she prayed. He walked in a day and a half later, angry at her. He had retrieved his messages from work; his mother had left him a message asking where he was. He was angry. Angry at her! He came in pissed off with her because she had called his mother and the police. He was angry; he was the one who stayed away from his wife, his home for a day and a half, telling no one where he went—and he was angry?

"What am I supposed to do?" she shouted back at him. "You went to work Friday and you come prancing in Sunday afternoon, like nothing has happened. I didn't know if you had been in an accident, hurt, or lying in some morgue dead. Where the hell were you! You should have called me," she screamed at him. He walked away from her, "Don't you ever call my mother again," he threw over his shoulder as he walked away. He never told her where he went, when he was going or when he would be back. She no longer worried about him. This time she was just tired.

She was tired of his disappearing act, she was tired of all the lies, she was tired of his begging and pleading on his knees with her not to divorce him, she was tired and she was stuck. Before God, their family and friends, she stood with him; they held hands and together he committed to give himself unto her only; to love her, to honor her and respect her, and to be there for each other, for life. He was a liar; he was not with her now. She did not want to be married to him anymore but she could not divorce him either. How could she change a commitment that she made to God first, then to her husband? How could she let go of the life that they had planned and imagined? How could she change her expectations, her viewpoint? She remembered what Momma Tee had told her, "Sometimes you need to move a little to the right or the left. Perhaps you need to take a step forward or a step backward to get a different view. And sometimes you may need to just put on someone else's shoes, try on their glasses to see life from their perspective." She did not know which way to move or where to look. She could not figure out what she did that was so wrong. She also recalled Momma Tee saying in her voice sweetened with Southern honey, "Sometimes when it rains it pours." Right then in her life it was pouring buckets.

The stress in her marriage had begun to show on her face; she felt weary in every cell of her body and she could not remember when she last slept through the night. Dark circles had appeared under her eyes and her eyes no longer sparkled with the joy of just being alive. She had put on weight. Eating temporarily numbed her, distracting her from the pain.

She and her husband had stopped having sex the second time that he disappeared. She couldn't do it; it was a breach of their agreement. In her mind he was disrespecting her, their vows, and their home. He was the one who came to her saying, "I want to be exclusive, just you and me." Those words fell from his mouth like snow. She did not know where he had been or where he was going. He could be bringing home cooties that he had gotten from some other person. The spread of HIV in the Black community was skyrocketing and he took no precautions. Her list of why his infidelity was so wrong was infinite.

The first time he stayed away, he came in apologizing for putting her through hell. Holding her hand he said, "I was wrong, I don't want to lose you." He came to her kissing away her tears, melting away her anger. He knew her, her body, and she surrendered, letting go, wanting to believe his words as she matched his passion. Two weeks later, he disappeared—again. He returned again, expecting to be forgiven, expecting that she would, as she had before, surrender in sex. He came back wanting to put that thing in her. She couldn't. It was just too nasty! It was clear to her that he did not care about her well-being; she would not endanger her health or her life, not even for him.

She told him, "No sex until you stop sleeping around. Then you need to take precautions until you get a clear

HIV test."

He laughed!

It was the last week of February, yellow and white daffodils were pushing through the cold soil and were standing in her garden, winter was winding down, spring was on the horizon and she was weary. She felt used up and worn out, so tired that just moving took great effort. She was stuck. And, she knew it! She called her longtime friend and confidant, Sherrie, and told her of her misery.

She was miserable. She knew she was on a merry-go-round but she did not know how to get off. She did not know how to move out of a commitment that she had made to life. She was tired. She knew she had to change.

It was Sherrie who invited her, she talked her into coming. She said, "Come to the party, dance, get out, you'll feel better."

She did not see him at first. It was his movements that caught her eye. He looked funny. His steps were unsteady. It seemed to her that each time he took a step his foot searched for the floor. He reminded her of an old Vaudeville performer pretending to be drunk. She could tell that this man was well into his cups. What she did not know at that time was that she was his destination.

They both belonged to the same social club. But that night was the first time he spoke to her, she and her husband had been members of the club since 1980. She had seen him around; her friends had pointed him out to her. Putting their lips close to her ear, they whispered, "See that man over there, he's a Nazi."

She looked where they pointed. She saw the man but didn't pay any attention to them or to him. He looked like a White man, an older White man with thin hair, silver white like the heads of towhead children. He stood about 5' 9" tall and his eyes were a startling, clear blue. He was not unique. He didn't have horns or a tail. He had no tattoos or other marks that would identify him as a Nazi. He looked like many other White men that she knew at the club and in the world.

When she realized that he was heading toward her, it was too late to move. Not tonight she prayed, not tonight. She was not in the mood tonight to talk to a drunk, especially one who was a Nazi. Her back was against the wall, he landed in front of her, stopping entirely too close. She could smell the unpleasant odor of alcohol mixed with food that has stayed too long in one's mouth. Leaning toward her he called her name and blew out, "Hello!" She was stunned, surprised, first because he spoke to her and then more so because he pronounced her name correctly.

"I am compelled to speak to you." He slurred, "I have hated N... all my life. I was born in Germany. I come from a family of Nazis. My father was a Nazi, my uncles are Nazis and today many of them are still active in the Klan. All of the things I was told about Blacks I have found to be true."

He swayed and slurred words tumbled out of his mouth. He said, "I know that Blacks are stupid, slow, and dim-witted and in fact that they are not even human. All my life I have worked toward the goal of White supremacy, doing everything necessary to keep Blacks, Jews, and Mexicans out of positions of power. I have spent my life keeping them in their place."

He went on, "I've seen you here at the club. I've watched you. My eyes follow you when you walk past and to my surprise many times when I come here, to the club, my eyes have sought you out. You are intelligent, articulate, smart, sociable, and attractive. There is something about you, an aura and an elegance that makes me want to know you. I don't know what to call it. I was confused at first," he said, "until I realized that you are different. You are different from other Blacks."

Her friend, Sherrie had come to stand near her and other friends had begun to gather around her, forming a protective circle, because they knew this man was a Nazi and they did not know his intent.

She did not say very much to him that night. Her thinking was clear enough to know that it is no use talking to a drunk. Her friends gathered close to her; she felt their hands on her shoulders and back, and she felt their protective love enfolding her.

As her friends moved closer, they asked her, "Are you alright, is everything well?"

They pulled her away from the wall, away from the Nazi. As she walked away, she turned, looking over her shoulder into the watery eyes of the drunken Nazi, and said, "I am no different from anyone else." The Nazi was left standing alone, rocking back and forth. She walked away thinking, "I hope someone drives him home."

She set her plastic glass of sour wine on a table and went home. Her husband was not there.

◆ ◆ ◆

A week! It was almost a week before her husband came home. She hesitated to call her home, the place where she lived, his home, because it was obvious to her that he had another place to rest his head, another place that was home. She mentioned divorce, but he did not want a divorce. He was adamant, on his knees. He pleaded with her, "Please, please don't divorce me!" He swore his love and promised not to not stray again. She left the room leaving him on his knees alone with his own words.

He had begun his habit of staying elsewhere after a dinner they had with their friends, Rocky and his wife, Ethel. He had invited them for dinner. It was Saturday night. They had all met each other at the club. They shared conversation and food and their children like each other. They were good people and she enjoyed their company.

She spent the day shopping and cooking. She really loved cooking and seeing people enjoying her food. Ethel and Rocky arrived on time and together they shared an excellent dinner and a wonderful bottle of wine. After dinner they retired to the living room with another bottle. There was something in the air; she had noticed it at dinner but did not understand what was going on. Another fifteen or twenty minutes passed, when Rocky said, "Oh, I need to get something from the store." He asked her to drive him.

As they drove away, Rocky asked her, "Your husband didn't tell you, did he?"

"Tell me what?" she asked.

Taking a deep breath, Rocky told her, "Ethel and I are swingers. We have sexual relationships with other couples but only when we are together." Her hands shook. She pulled over to the curb, shaking her head and trying to make sense of what she had just heard, looking at Rocky, she asked, "What?"

Rocky repeated what he said. Her hands continued to shake. Her palms were sweaty. He placed his hand over hers and said, "It's OK!"

She couldn't speak; she couldn't understand how he, her husband, the man she committed to keep herself only unto him could have set up an intimate meeting, a sexual exchange without talking to her, without considering her feelings. She felt that the world has just shifted out of focus. It took a long time before she felt steady enough to drive again. When they got back to her home, Rocky took Ethel's hand and they left.

She could barely get the words out of her mouth. The questions came so quickly, she stuttered, "How could you do this, how could you not ask me if this is what I wanted?"

Her husband walked away asking, "What's the big deal?"

That Friday was the first time that he stayed away overnight.

◆ ◆ ◆

It was one of the last hot days of Indian summer, 1986. She was worn and exhausted it was the weekend. What she wanted was to be comforted; what she needed was to be held; what she sought was a retreat. She went to the club to lie in the sun and let it bake the pain away. She wanted a massage and a sauna. It was in the sauna when the Nazi spoke to her again.

The small hot sauna room was crowded. The only available seat was next to her. The Nazi entered, looked at the empty seat next to her and turned a complete circle looking for another place, after completing the circle he stopped when he came to her again. Cocking his head a little he asked her, "Do you mind sitting next to a White man?"

She shook her head no, asking him, "Do you mind sitting next to a Black woman?"

He spread his towel next to hers and sat down. Raising her eyes she saw her friend Bob looking at her and shaking his head, "No!" She chuckled, because she was the only person of color in the sauna and her friend Bob was warning her off, not to say anything to the Nazi.

They all sat in silence. People came and went until there were only three of them left sitting and sweating.

The Nazi began pulling and twisting and untwisting his fingers. When his fingers were still he began, "My father was always a difficult man; but was more difficult, meaner, and much more violent after he got out of prison. He was a soldier in World War II, a member of Hitler's army. He served until the war was finished."

"He was arrested and put on trial for crimes he was accused of committing during the war. They said it was his friends that reported him. He went to prison."

"My mother and I were shunned. Our friends would not speak to us, children I used to play with teased and harassed me. The only work my mother could get was cleaning a bakery that belonged to people she knew. She was paid very little, just enough to rent a little room with one bed. At night, after the bakery closed, she swept up the flour that had spilled on the floor. She swept it up and it brought home and made bread for us to eat. It was a long time before I could eat baked goods without feeling the grit of dirt."

"When my father was released from prison, he moved us to Canada."

As she sat in the sauna and listened to the Nazi's story, she thought it interesting that he selected the sauna, a small, hot enclosed box, where people go to sweat out the toxins, the impurities from our bodies, to have this conversation. He sat for a while after telling this story. Without saying another word he stood up, took his towel, and left the sauna.

◆ ◆ ◆

The sun was hot that summer in 1987 when he spoke to her again. It was late afternoon and the shadows were growing long. She was sitting on the deck at the club, reading, when he approached her. He sat down next to her, he said hello and started talking, talking as if they were in the middle of an ongoing conversation.

"You don't understand," he said, "there is a reason why I feel this way about Blacks. In my youth I had a terrible, traumatic experience involving Blacks."

The Nazi continued speaking as if they were continuing an unfinished conversation, and, with his head down, he told her this story.

"My father moved us to Canada. We had family in Alabama—uncles, aunts, and cousins. Each year my father sent me to spend the summer with them. I was the oldest and my younger cousins looked up to me. The year I turned sixteen I got my driver's license. I was the only one who could drive. It was really cool. My uncle let me drive his car and introduced me to his friends with pride in his voice. It was the best, because I was treated like a man. I was respected and I could drive my cousins and our friends anywhere we wanted to go. I was important; they liked me.

I was driving through town. It was hot and it was muggy. We had just finished a game of baseball and I was driving us into town to the local market to get ice cold NeHi Sodas. Heading toward home, I stopped at the corner to let a woman and a young boy cross the street. Immediately, my cousins and their friends began to yell and curse me. They began hitting me about my head, shoulders, and back. Family members—cousins and friends that I had known for years—turned to me with faces distorted with distaste! They called me foul, degrading, demeaning, and humiliating names. The breath went out of my chest, I couldn't breathe. They threw the sharp NeHi bottle caps at me. One even cut me, here." he pointed, "over my eye". Their voices, usually open and warm, had turned cruel and brutal. They encouraged me, challenged me, and dared me to run over the woman and the small child. 'Run them over,' they hissed at me, 'no one's going to miss them. Their kin like them are not even human. They don't feel things the way we do.' My cousins razzed me, hit and punched me, chided me and called me those horrible names just because I stopped to let a woman and child cross the street."

"They made my visit that summer so very uncomfortable. I was so humiliated, so shamed that I went home early that summer. When I got home, my uncle had called my father and told him what I had done. I regretted going home. My father was worse than they were, much worse. My cousins teased me for years. If I were to go visit them today, they would still torment me, calling me foul names."

"You see," he turned his head to look at me staring into my eyes; "the woman and the young boy that I stopped to let cross the street were Black."

She was stunned. "That is your horrible experience with Blacks?" She almost screamed at him! "I have friends who were punched, hit, and spat on by Whites, by racists. A friend told me how his father was dragged from his house by men dressed in white. They tied his hands and his feet, threw a rope over his head, and dragged him behind their truck. They did this because his father refused to cross the street when a White man told him to 'get off the sidewalk!'"

She threw words at him. The Nazi drew in, as if shrinking into himself to get away from her.

When she saw him shrink away from her, retreating into himself like a wounded animal, she stopped. She saw herself, she saw that she had become like those people whose story he just shared. Taking a deep breath, leaning forward she placed her hand on his arm, her eyes met his, "I'm so sorry that you had to go through that," she said. You see, it was her commitment, her pledge not to harm others with her thoughts, words and actions. She could see clearly that the words that she flung at the Nazi harmed him.

When the Nazi spoke of his experience, she could see the pain in his eyes and hear the ache in his voice. She remembered what it was like to be sixteen, desperately needing to be liked. She had not grown up in an abusive home so it was hard to imagine his childhood and his relationship with his father. But she understood the pain that he felt; she knew what it felt like needing to be liked. She also understood that his attitude toward people of African Heritage and Jews were all tied up with his pain. His story was that his father went to prison because of Jews. His story was that his life was hard, full of pain because of people of Jewish and African descent. It was because of them—others—that his father was so brutally cruel. His loss of face, respect with his cousins and their friends was because of Blacks. In his mind, in his life, his story was that his pain was caused by others. That was the story he chose to believe, and that was the story that he lived, it was the story that became his life.

Her thoughts were disturbed. As she drove home, she thought about the story that the Nazi shared. The comparisons were so apparent—between the stories of denigration and pain that the Nazi experienced and the stories of denigration and pain that she knew her foremothers and forefathers suffered at the hands of racists. She knew that there were many people who would judge his experience differently, as she had initially. Just as her ancestors suffered, so did this tortured man. She went to sleep that night with a prayer for peace for the Nazi and people everywhere.

She woke up the next morning alone.

◆ ◆ ◆

Most of the winter of 1987-1988 was a blur. She and the Nazi had seen each other over that winter. It was always with others; they shared dinner in groups of mutual friends. They spoke but those conversations did not linger in her mind. Sitting in front of the fire, they played her favorite board game, Scrabble. She found that in playing games he was as competitive as she. It seemed that they were well matched. When she was victor, she jumped up and did a jig; when he won all he required was a high-five! There is a closeness that comes when playing games; locked in a battle of luck and strategy, in that battle they grew closer.

It was summer 1988 when she and her husband separated. She lived alone and he moved in with the woman he was seeing. Struggling in her mind about being married but living alone made her weary. Her husband told her it was her fault that he stayed away; she could make the marriage work if she did what he wanted. She was agitated, frustrated, and angry. She really wanted to scream, nothing she said got through to her husband. Even though she initiated the separation, she felt like a failure. She had cried enough tears to fill the two oceans and still tears continued to fall. Peace seemed impossible. She took off work and went to the club to rest and to sweat in the sauna. It was Friday. Her intention was to lie in the sun and allow it to draw all the pain from her body.

Sitting on the upper lawn, baking in the summer sun, she sat reading. It was one of those novels by an acclaimed writer, an engaging story of people overcoming unearthly obstacles to gain peace. She didn't see him approach. When she looked up from her book he was there, sitting on the grass next to her. He sat cross-legged. He was reading also. This time he was silent. When he saw her looking at him, he smiled. It seemed that he didn't need to talk; it was like he just needed to be near her.

Instead of listening, this time she spoke. She poured out stories that have been passed from grandmother to granddaughter for generations. She told him the story of Phoebe's mother. She told the Nazi how Phoebe's mother was kidnapped from her home, her family, her community, and everything that she knew. Her hands were tied and her feet shackled and was made to walk dozens of countless miles to the coast of Africa where she was thrown into the dark belly of a ship with hundreds of other people, made to lie head to toe, head to toe to endure a voyage, called the middle passage, that she could not imagine.

That day he received the brunt of her frustration though the stories and struggles of her distant relatives. It had not been her intention to dump her frustration on him. He sat and listened to her family stories and tears appeared in the corner of his eye as he listened to how Phoebe and Mike's family was torn apart in the hands of racists. He heard and felt the pride she had for her great-grandmother, Susie Edwards. Susie was a small brown woman who faced the cloaked phantoms alone and sent them shrieking into the night. He could see that this woman was a giant in the teller's eyes. She shared with him the foundational principle that has been an inspiration for her family: the impossible can be made possible. When she finished, she closed her eyes as she slumped back in her lounge chair, spent. He sat with her a while in the silence. When she opened her eyes he was gone.

That night after a sauna and dinner at the club, she went home and slept through the entire night.

◆ ◆ ◆

Their meetings were not intentional; at least not on her part. Sometimes seasons passed between their conversations and there were other times when they spoke two or three or four days running. If she was taking her daily walk in the hills or on the club grounds, sometimes he walked with her and they talked. Most of those conversations did not stay with her. It was simply two people walking or climbing the hill puffing out words between breaths. Other times when he would see her sitting alone and he would join her and begin talking, the way he always did, starting right in, like he was keeping a running record of their conversations in his head, like time had not passed since they last spoke.

Over time other stories flowed from each of them. From the Nazi there were stories of pain, abuse, and humiliation that left him unclear as to who he was. He told her that he could not reach his mother after they moved to Canada, she became small; he said it was like she ran away inside of herself. He told her that he did not know why he was drawn to her, a Black woman. He said he had simply asked for peace so he surrendered and followed where his heart and head told him to go. From her there were stories of her great-grandfather William James Edwards, a pioneer who, in the early 1800's established a normal college, Snow Hill Institute of Technology for African Americans. She shared with the Nazi stories of pain and anguish that her ancestors and her family experienced at the hands of racists. She also shared with him the vision, courage, commitment, and faith of her ancestors; their triumphs over adversity and her own victory over hate and the transformation of hate to compassion then to love that was her salvation. And she told him of the ache that she still carried from her experiences with overt racism, an ache which flared when she saw or heard of injustices done to others, regardless of their color, culture, or faith tradition.

And, they found that they could make the other laugh!

He had a way of looking at her when she spoke. He did not interrupt and he did not ask questions; he simply sat and listened. His startlingly blue eyes were piercing, looking inside her. Sometimes she felt uncomfortable under his piercing stare. She asked him once, "What are you looking at, why do you stare at me so intensely? What are you looking for?"

"I am looking at the real you," He replied.

Smiling, she asked him if he had found her. Looking into her eyes, "I think so," he said.

It was months now; her husband came home once in a while. Most of the time she did not see him, but she knew he had come because there were wet towels hanging in the bathroom and dirty clothes in the hamper. Once she woke up and found him stretched out on the living room sofa; "we had an argument", he told her. After that she changed the locks. She still was not sleeping. Her health deteriorated. Migraines and high blood pressure threatened her health. Her doctor told her, "Cut back at work, drop out of school. I can't tell you how serious the risk to your health is if you do not change what you are doing," Her doctor warned her, but she was not ready.

The Nazi and she were over two years into their conversation, when she asked him, "How many people of African Heritage have you spoken to? What kind of interactions have you had with people of color?"

Twisting and pulling on his fingers and looking at the ground, he said, "None!" He cocked his head a little to the right and looking at her kind of sideways he said, "You are the first." He went on to tell her that there was a Black man where he worked; they had worked in the same area for many years but had never had a conversation, they nodded at each other in passing, but they never spoke.

"You are the first Black person that I ever initiated a conversation with; you are the first that I ever wanted to speak with."

She was stunned; again, she almost shouted, "You made up your mind; you made judgments about an entire group of people and you have never even talked to any of them! You have never had a conversation with a person of African heritage or even an interaction, yet you acted on stories that you heard, stories that you did not even explore to see if they were true?"

For a while, the Nazi looked at her. Then he dropped his eyes and began pulling and twisting his fingers.

She took a deep breath. She could see his confusion, his struggle. Her anger evaporated as she came to understand the step that he had taken in speaking with her. She understood the courage that it had taken him to approach her for the first time. She remembered how drunk he had been. In his quest for Truth, he had allowed her a window into his life. His beliefs, attitudes, and actions were all tied up with his pain—and he could not separate them. She told him that she was glad that something in her compelled him to speak to her. What she did not say was that it was a beginning for both of them.

She did not remember when she told the Nazi about her husband and her marriage. She disclosed to him that she felt like a failure, even though she had done everything, except agree to the type of marriage that her husband wanted. She was not judgmental about her husband's choice; it just was not the type of relationship that she wanted. She told the Nazi that she did not want to be married to her husband anymore, but was stuck because she made a commitment, to God, to herself and to her husband, "until death do us part."

The man who she had called a Nazi, looked at her in that way and said, "Even though I've never been married," he said, "I've always understood the words, until death do us part, to mean until the death of the marriage, not the death of the human body." He went on, "If you continue to live with a dead thing it will begin to rot—infecting you and all those around you. If you do not physically die immediately, you will die spiritually; you will shrivel up and become a dried thing and life will flee from your presence."

She was startled by his words. She remembered her head jerking up and looking into his eyes. The clear blue of his eyes had become prism of colors made by his unshed tears.

Then he said, "My mother lived in that type of marriage and she died long before her body gave out."

She reached her hand out to him. He took her hand in his.

◆ ◆ ◆

Over time she began to understand that the stories that people believe, the stories that people choose to believe, became their lives. The Nazi had been trained from childhood to hate others. She believed that kind of hate eats away at a person, either completely consuming them or catapulting them to a new awareness. She also saw the stories in her own life. She saw that the stories she believed dictated her choices, and she saw that the stories that she believed became her life.

She knew that there were times when he sought her out; he told her so. There were times when he would sit next to her, each reading or resting being in each other's presence. Times when they would smile, speak, and inquire how the other's life was going. To her, he was always respectful and she was to him, in return.

She remembered the first time they danced. It was at the club. She invited him to dance; he accepted. The first dance was one of those fast dances and they laughed at each other's style. Her invitation opened the door. After that he felt free to ask her to dance. He did and they did dance. She remembered feeling uncomfortable in her mind, when he first asked her to dance to a slow song. It wasn't the first time that they touched, but she could feel his hands trembling, the one that held her hand and the one he put at her back. She could feel his breath on her cheek, on her neck, and in her hair. As they moved around the floor, he whispered in her ear, "thank you for being you."

She and this man continued a conversation that spanned years. She was reticent to say that they became close buddies, and she was uncomfortable saying that they were friends. They did not talk on the phone or hang out together or go places together. They were acquaintances and more. She realized, even then, that they shared an intimacy that many people who were married years did not share. She never told anyone about their conversations, she had a hint that this journey was important to each of them. They shared a closeness where all pretenses were dropped, an understanding and trust that their confidences were held as sacred conversations. Not judged—they were accepted. She certainly felt closer to him than to her husband. She felt closer to him than some she had known for years. She never asked him how he held their conversations, but the times when she would look up and see him sitting near her, feeling her gaze upon him; he would look up and smile. They did not always talk and later, much later when she saw him in at the club in the restaurant alone, she would sit with him and they would share a meal, sometimes talking other times simply being in the other's company. She searched a long time for a word that described what was held between them, "confessors" was the word she settled on. It was years into their conversation when he told her that he found comfort in her presence.

They met at a time when they were both poised for change. The Universe had aligned itself for them to meet; they took the steps toward a conversation. They began by listening to each other. They learned to hear beyond the words and they came to understand that the pain they both felt from life was the same. They talked about pain that people inflicted upon one another. They talked about pain that people inflicted upon themselves and they talked about growth. They were able to share pain and redemption, tears and laughter, meals and conversation, and together they walked into the unknown, together they walked into possibility. She did not realize it at that time, a conversation, intimacy between a Nazi and an African woman—the impossible made possible!

◆ ◆ ◆

It was late in the summer of 1991 when their conversation ended where it had begun, in the sauna. The small hot room was crowded. He walked in the only available seat was next to her. He turned to her with a smile, his eyes sparkling and asked, "Do you mind sitting next to a White man?" Looking up she smiled back and answered, "Do you mind sitting next to a Black woman?" He spread his towel and sat down. He said, "No." Looking into each others eyes, they both laughed. The others in the sauna gave them a strange look.

They sat in silence. One by one people took their leave until there was only the two of them left sweating. She noticed that when he first walked in he appeared uncomfortable. He sat next to her, looking down and began pulling, twisting, and untwisting his fingers. She had learned over time that the twisting, untwisting, and pulling on his fingers meant that he had something to say. She waited. Time passed. She did not know how much time had passed when he began, "I don't know if this means anything to you. I don't know if you will even care, but I am again compelled to speak to you; to say this to you."

His fingers went still. He sat with his palms up and he said, "I am sorry for what White people have done to Black people over all these years."

Again, he began twisting and untwisting his fingers, and time passed. He raised his head and looked at her. His eyes were full. She could not tell if the wetness on his cheeks was tears or sweat from sitting in the hot box. Looking at her with his voice shaking, he said, "I am sorry, I am so sorry for the part that I played. I am so sorry for the things I said and so sorry for the things I did."

In the hot sauna, sweating, sitting there shoulder to shoulder, she could not tell if her checks were wet from tears or the cleansing sweat from sitting in the dry heat. She looked at him, opened her hand, and he laid his hand in hers and said very softly she said, "Thank you."

Then she shared a prayer with him, a prayer that Momma Tee whispered in the ears of new born babies: "Life is whatever you make it to be. You have choice. You can be whatever you choose, because you are Spirit."

They sat together well after his sobs ceased.

They sat side by side in the hot room, sweating. She again noted that they were in the sauna, the place where people go to sweat the toxins and impurities from their bodies. She wondered if saunas also sweated the toxins and the impurities from their souls. As they sat shoulder to shoulder, she realized that they both had moved into possibility.

◆ ◆ ◆

She saw her husband shortly after that and told him to move the rest of his things out of her house. The next morning she set up interviews with the paralegals and before the sun went down that day she had filed the necessary papers. She had changed her story about her marriage; her divorce became final in February, 1992.

◆ ◆ ◆

It was a Wednesday night, the summer after her divorce was finalized—she does not remember the date—when the man who first introduced himself to her as a Nazi—came to her in her dreams. He was standing like she had seen him so many times before, peering at her with those startlingly clear blue eyes like he was looking inside her at her soul. Calling her name, he gently spoke to her, "Thank you," he began, "because of your willingness, your openness, and your unconditional acceptance of me I can now move onward to the next level. I am grateful to you beyond words, beyond all life. I leave this story as our legacy." Then he was gone.

She had never really thought about this man very much beyond their conversations. She had never considered his affiliation a threat and she certainly never dreamed about him. She knew that their conversations moved her, opened a door, shining a light where before there was darkness. She also knew that their conversations moved him. Still, it was a surprise when he showed up in her dreams. For two more nights he came to her, each time saying the same thing.

On Saturday of that week, she was having dinner with friends. Half way through the evening, the husband of the couple looked at her said, "Oh, did you know that the Nazi died?" His wife quickly added, "Yes, he passed away early Wednesday. They think it was a heart attack."

She froze. Her fork slipped to the table. She could hardly speak, turning pale. She flashed back on what the man had said to her in her dreams and then on something that Momma Tee said, "Life is whatever you make it to be, the impossible can be made possible."

Her friends, their voices full of concern, asked her, "What's the matter?"

She told them this story. . .

An Afterword
Whispered Blessings

In some traditions, it is believed that newly born babies have just come from the place that their grandparents will soon return and that the babies bring messages from the other side to the grandparent reminding them of home to make their transition back easier.

It is also believed that children who grow up without grandparents grow up damaged, because it is necessary for the grandparent to whisper a blessing in the ear of newly born baby; a blessing reminding the baby of their own unique divinity, preparing the baby for this world.

This is the tradition that Momma Tee carries forward. ❧

Momma Tee
Whispered Blessings

With vision, courage, commitment, and faith,
the impossible can be made possible.

—Momma Tee

Tee was outrageous. She was regal. When she entered a room, all eyes shifted their focus to her. She was grace, serenity, elegance, and peace. Tee wore hats and she sometimes wrapped herself in yards and yards of fabric. She would wrap fabric around her head, letting it flow down her back like a waterfall, or she would twist it and twirl it around her body so that when she spread her arms she looked like a great, beautiful, colorful bird perched for flight. I remember seeing her walk through the house and snatch a furniture doily off the piano. She stuck it in her hat and off she went to church. Her brother-in-law once described her as "gaudy, with a classic sort of elegance." She never dressed according to fashion but she was always fashionable. Friends and family members often speak of seeing a hat, fabric, or jewelry saying, "Ah, that's Tee's style."

When she was well past the half century mark, her skin— the color of freshly roasted coffee beans—was smooth. Her back was straight and her body was firm.

A healer, a blesser of babies, a blower of bubbles, and the teller of wondrous stories, Momma Tee is the embodiment of all the women that I admire, respect, honor, and love.

Momma Tee is like that jigsaw puzzle piece that never seems to fit anywhere but belongs everywhere. She has the ability to make anyone feel comfortable. I have heard stories of how children have been known to make remarkable recoveries and adults to exclaim "I feel refreshed," after spending time in Tee's company. I heard people use the words magic, voodoo; but they went to see Tee when they or their loved ones fell ill. "Witch," others called. She didn't talk much about her gift of healing at least not to me anyway. "Life is magic," she said. "People just forget that life is a magical, mystical, divine gift. The real magic is our Creator's unbounded, unconditional love."

People did talk about her. They chatted to each other about how she dressed. They talked about the way she referred to God as "She"! One of the first to wear her hair in dread locks; she wore them hanging down her back or tied up in a crown resting securely on her head. I passed the church ladies one Sunday after service, I heard them talking about Tee. "After her second husband died," they whispered. "She's past 80," they said, "She takes lovers half her age", another almost shouted. When they saw me, they waved their hands at me, shooing me way. Tee lived life fully, passionately, following the perennial philosophy and remembering a whispered blessing.

I heard people say, "Tee's doesn't have on shoes." She was barefoot at the podium, on the dais, and in the pulpit. Barefoot, she gave keynote addresses, participated in rituals and celebrations, lectured at the university, talked stories, and in sacred spaces she invited those present to join her in sacred conversations—barefoot.

And, when she became a minister; people talked about her, a woman who many think sometimes lived her life outside of the rules. Some questioned her worthiness for the sacred title of minister, not knowing that their thoughts and words showed on their faces and in their voices. Others protested, exclaiming, "How is that possible; do you know that she . . . ! And, she also . . .?" Tee paid no attention to what people said about her. "People will talk about you no matter what you do or no matter what you don't do. Life was too short to care what people say about me." "But, sometimes," Tee smiled, "I want to give them something good to talk about!"

She used to call those experiences, "between the rock and the hard place" Those times and in those places when our nature appeared to be at conflict with its Self. "There were times when I really want to say something, to protest their criticism; to hold up a mirror. But I know that if I respond, if I claim justification, if I point a finger at them for what they are doing and saying—I know that at that moment, at that moment I have become just like them." She now calls those times, "The Divine giving me an opportunity to practice being what I said I want to be, peace and love"

Her faith grew out of her experience. "I give gratitude for this gift of now, gratitude for the sacrifices and the triumphs of my ancestors. I live in gratitude with the Holy Spirit, when I remember that the breath of God lives in me as me I just want to shout with joy."

Tee stood as straight and as tall as a palm tree. She told people that she was 5'8" tall. They believed her. That is until they stood next to her and looked down upon the top her head, sparkling with threads of silver. Momma Tee said that she had perfected the illusion of a very tall, strong, powerful woman. The only illusion was her height. You see, she really was only five feet tall.

Even when she reached a great old age, her ebony skin was smooth with undertones of red, gold, and green. Her sparkling black eyes stood out—the focal point of her face—that reminded me of the August moon against the dark sky. If her eyes were the moon, then her face became the sun when she smiled; she radiated light. Her deep, hearty laugh was contagious, filling the space until the room rang from the sheer joy of the sound.

We called her Momma Tee. My mother told me this was because when she became a "woman," she began to call herself by a name that was too difficult for her young nieces and nephews to pronounce. So, she gave them permission— permission mind you—to call her "Auntie Tee." When her only son had children they called her Momma Tee. So it began.

Momma Tee said, "Gratitude naturally arises from remembrance and gratitude leads us to celebrate. Sometimes, I just want to dance, sing, and shout my love and gratitude for life to everyone!"

She said, "What I say is not unique. I certainly am not the first and I won't be the last person who says this: it does not matter what path you choose, if you live by one principle, let it be treat others as you would like to be treated." For this, people talked about her. And, they talked about her because she always barefoot.

Tee lived by a perennial philosophy that is found in all faith traditions that are grounded in justice and compassion: "That which is harmful, that which is distasteful, that which is not delightful to you, do not do to another" or said another way "do unto other as you would have them do unto you."

When I remember Momma Tee, I see her in hats with yards of fabric trailing behind her. I see her as daughter, sister, mother, aunt, friend, artist, dancer, teacher, leader, healer, blower of bubbles, and teller of the most wondrous stories. But, what I remember most of all about Momma Tee was that she was a blesser of babies.

Whenever a baby was born in the community Tee would make sure to hold it. She would take the newly born baby in her arms and say, "Welcome, welcome to this life; welcome to this world little one."

Then she asked the baby, "What messages do you bring Momma Tee?" Placing her ear close to the baby's lips, she would nod her head and sometimes she would smile, as she received the baby's message. You see, in some ancient communities, it is believed that babies come from a place in which the grandparent would soon return. And, that the baby brings messages to the grandparent, reminding them of the world that they would soon return.

Placing her lips close to the baby's ear she would begin blessing the baby:

Walk tall, straight and be strong.
Use your inner site to see what is really real,
Do not be swayed from your path.
Remain true to yourself.
Live long, love deeply, laugh a lot and remember . . .

Breathing deeply she continued:

Life is whatever you make it to be, the choice is yours.
This life is a gift from the most High and you;
Your thoughts, words and actions are gifts in return
You can be what ever you want to be.
You can make the impossible possible
Because you are Spirit.

Bowing her head over the baby, she whispered,

You are a gift from God
and you are a gift to God.
Remember!

Tee then blessed the baby with wisdom, and advised the baby to use compassion and love in all her choices. She whispered in the baby's ear. "Remember" she would say, handing the child back to its parents, "Remember."

Momma Tee started blessing babies when she was a young woman, when she saw that no one was blessing the babies and providing a welcome for them into this world. When she saw that no one was reminding the babies—and thus ourselves—that, "We decide what our life will be, the choice is ours" and that "Life is a gift from God and that we, our thoughts, words, and actions are our gifts to God. It is the ultimate in loving and giving, when the gift given becomes a gift to the giver."

In the bustling cosmopolitan society, this world community in which we all live, people had forgotten their customs, their traditions, their rituals, people had forgotten their stories. She began blessing babies, quietly at first, because she was concerned about what people would think and say about what she did. But as more people forgot their stories and as the world began to sink further and further into chaos and madness, she cared less what people thought about her and more about the lives that the babies would live tomorrow. So she began blessing babies.

Tee found that the many faith traditions and beliefs held a central core. Combining all and representing none and remembering a whispered blessing she began to bless babies. The color, the religion, the culture, the sex, the location did not matter. The blessing of the baby was always the same:

Walk tall, straight and be strong.
Use your inner sight to see what is really real.
Do not be swayed from your path.
Remain true to yourself.
Live long, love deeply, laugh a lot and remember . . .

Life is whatever you make it to be, the choice is yours.
This life is a gift from the most High and you.
Your thoughts, words and actions are gifts in return.
You can be whatever you want to be,
You can make the impossible, possible,
Because you are Spirit.
Remember! Remember!

In her middle years, Momma Tee began to travel the world collecting and sharing stories. Momma Tee said, "Sharing stories is my way of making a difference." She said, "People listen to stories with their ears, but they hear them with their heart."

She found that no matter where she went in the world; whether it be a large metropolis, a small town, or a village; she found that all people want the same thing. Everyone wants to live in peace. All people want to raise their children in a safe, secure community surrounded with love. And, everyone wants a better life for their children tomorrow, than they have today. But, Tee found that somehow we have forgotten how to love, how to honor and how respect each other. We have forgotten how to honor, respect and to love life. We have forgotten our traditions, our history, we have forgotten our stories. Momma Tee said, "A people without stories become lost in the unknown."

A teacher, a blower of bubbles, a healer, a teller of wondrous stories, and a blesser of babies, Momma Tee told me to remind you that:

Life is whatever you make it to be, the choice is yours.
This life is a gift from the most High and you.
Your thoughts, words and actions are gifts in return.
You can be whatever you want to be,
You can make the impossible, possible,
Because you are Spirit.
Remember!

Remember!

Breinigsville, PA USA
21 April 2010
236536BV00001B/4/P